The New Chicks

Written by Michèle Dufresne
Illustrated by Cula Carmen Elena

Contents

Chapter 1 • Eggs at Home 2

Chapter 2 • The Growing Chicks 12

Pioneer Valley Educational Press, Inc.

CHAPTER ONE
Eggs at Home

Little Penguin went to look
for Mother Penguin. He found her
sitting on a nest. "I need help
with my homework," he told her.

"I'm busy," Mother Penguin replied.
"Your father can help you
when he returns. He's out fishing at sea."

"What are you doing?" asked Little Penguin.

"I'm sitting on my new eggs,"
his mother answered. She stood up
and showed Little Penguin the two eggs
in her nest.

"Why are you sitting on the eggs?"
asked Little Penguin.

"To keep them warm,"
replied Mother Penguin.
"Soon you will have two new brothers
or sisters."

Little Penguin frowned and said,
"I don't want any brothers or sisters!"

"You will like having brothers
or sisters to play with,"
said his mother. "You'll see."

The next day, Little Penguin
went to find his friend, Baby Seal.
"I don't want any brothers or sisters,"
Little Penguin told Baby Seal.
"All my mother and father
talk about are those silly eggs.
No one pays any attention to me."

"You'll like having brothers
or sisters. I like playing with
my big brother," said Baby Seal.
"You'll see. It'll be fun."

One day, when Little Penguin came home from fishing, there were no longer two eggs in Mother Penguin's nest. Instead, there were two fuzzy, gray chicks.

"Squawk!" said one.

"Squawk! Squawk!" said the other.

Mother Penguin came over to the nest carrying a basket of fish. "Did you meet your new brothers?" she asked as she started feeding the chicks.

"They're funny looking," said Little Penguin.

"Soon, they will shed their soft, gray feathers and grow new feathers just like yours," Mother Penguin told Little Penguin. "We need to take care of them because they are too young to be by themselves. But soon, you'll be able to have lots of fun playing with them."

"Humph," said Little Penguin as he turned and walked away.

CHAPTER TWO
The Growing Chicks

The two chicks grew and grew.
Soon they started following Little Penguin
everywhere. Whenever he went fishing,
they wanted to go. And whenever
he went exploring, they wanted to go, too.

One day, Little Penguin and Baby Seal
decided to go sledding.

"Please, can we go with you?"
begged the two chicks.

"Oh, all right," said Little Penguin.
"But we are not carrying you. You must
walk the whole way by yourselves!"

The two chicks followed
Baby Seal and Little Penguin.
They pulled their little, blue sled
along behind them.

"You can slide here
on this small hill," said Little Penguin.
"We'll be over there on that big hill."
He pointed to a big hill in the distance.

"Can't we come with you?"
begged one of the chicks.

"No!" answered Little Penguin.

Baby Seal whispered to Little Penguin,
"The big hill is pretty far away."

"Good," said Little Penguin.
"Those chicks are annoying! They're
always following me around!"

Little Penguin and Baby Seal
went up and down the big hill
over and over again.
Little Penguin forgot all about his brothers.

Then they heard, "Help! Help!"

"Little Penguin, I think
I hear your brothers," said Baby Seal.
"It sounds like they're calling
from the sea!"

"Oh, no!" said Little Penguin.
"They *are* annoying, but
I don't want anything bad
to happen to them."

"I know you don't," replied his friend.

Baby Seal and Little Penguin jumped onto their sled and slid down the big hill toward the sea.

When they got to the sea, Little Penguin and Baby Seal looked down and saw the two chicks floating on their sled in the water. Little Penguin lowered a rope down to the chicks. "Hold on to the rope, and we will pull you up," he called.

Little Penguin and Baby Seal pulled and pulled and pulled the two chicks up onto the bank.

The chicks hugged Little Penguin. "You saved us!" they cried. "You are the best big brother in the whole wide world."

"No, I'm not," sighed Little Penguin.
"But I promise I'll be a better brother
from now on. Hop on the sled
and we'll pull you up the big hill.
We can all go sledding together."